Geo
ANIMAL FARM

Ralph Ranald

Assistant Dean, Liberal Arts College
New York University

Laurie Rozakis, Ph.D.

The State University of New York
at Farmingdale

BARNES
&NOBLE
BOOKS
NEW YORK

The publisher of ANIMAL FARM is Harcourt, Brace & World, Inc.

Copyright © 1997, 1965 by Simon & Schuster, Inc.

This edition published by Barnes & Noble, Inc.,
by arrangement with Macmillan Publishing USA,
a division of Simon & Schuster, Inc.

1997 Barnes & Noble Books

MACMILLAN is a registered trademark of Macmillan, Inc.
Monarch and colophons are trademarks of Simon & Schuster, Inc.,
registered in the U.S. Patent and Trademark Office.

Macmillan Publishing USA
A division of Simon & Schuster, Inc.
1633 Broadway
New York, NY 10019

ISBN 0-7607-0558-5

Text design by Tony Meisel

Printed and bound in the United States of America.

97 98 99 00 01 M 9 8 7 6 5 4 3 2 1

RRDC

CONTENTS

GEORGE ORWELL

In 1943, likely the most hopeless year of the twentieth century for Western civilization, George Orwell published an essay called "Looking Back on the Spanish War." Orwell had served as a volunteer in the Spanish Civil War, which took place from 1936 to 1939. Orwell met the subject of the poem, an anonymous soldier, at the start of the war. The soldier stands for all the ordinary soldiers who fought in Spain's destructive Civil War.

The last stanza of the poem sheds light on Orwell the man and Orwell the writer. Here is how Orwell addresses this unknown soldier at the end of the poem: "But the thing that I saw in your face No power can disinherit: No bomb that ever burst, shatters the crystal spirit."

The line "No bomb that ever burst, shatters the crystal spirit" could stand for George Orwell's own life and what he stood for: the dignity of humanity, the inviolability of the human spirit, and each person's right to spiritual privacy. According to our Declaration of Independence, people have "certain inalienable rights," and it is the inalienability of these rights which Orwell affirmed in all his works. Consequently, it is a paradox that Orwell's deservedly great reputation today rests primarily on *1984* and *Animal Farm,* two works which seem to express the deepest pessimism about human nature. But the conflict between Orwell's seeming pessimism and optimism can be reconciled by study of his biography and his writings.

EARLY YEARS

George Orwell was born Eric Arthur Blair in 1903 in Motihari, Bengal, an area in eastern India only about three hundred miles from Burma, where Orwell was to serve twenty years later as a British civil servant. He was the only son of a subordinate British civil servant; his father, serving in the British Raj (government) of India, worked in the Customs and Excise department. Apparently Orwell's father was reserved and distant with his children. Orwell had a sister about five years older than he, and another five years younger, but he was never very close to his sisters either. Indeed, by his own account he was close only to his mother. This attitude is revealed in what Orwell said about his early childhood in his famous essay "Such, Such Were the Joys . . ." which deals with his unhappy career at an English preparatory school.

As a salaried official without an independent income, Orwell's father was not well off financially. The family's financial difficulties haunted Orwell. For example, on one occasion Orwell described the social class into which he was born as "lower upper-middle," perhaps with a touch of irony at such attempts at precise classification. Many of Orwell's essays and novels contain references to social class and social distinction.

EDUCATION

In 1911, Orwell was sent back to England to begin his education. These were the last quiet years of the pre-World War I era, when the imperial power of England was unquestioned. As a result, the government required a constant supply of young men who would learn the art and science of ruling in England and then relocate to India, Burma, and other far reaches of the British Empire to staff the government offices. And such a career—his father's—seems at this point to have been Orwell's destiny. Thus, the lengthy enforced separation from his family—there was certainly not enough money for the boy to make visits back to India—followed the expected pattern among the English middle- and upper-middle classes.

The educational system, based on a rigid class structure, had narrow but clearly defined goals. This system had a profound effect on Orwell, coloring much of his writing and actions. The preparatory school he attended beginning at age eight was located on the southern coast of England; it is the school to which he referred, though not by its actual name, in the essay "Such, Such Were the Joys . . . ." This essay is a bitter attack on the kind of education which was respected among the middle and upper classes in Great Britain. Orwell was a boarding student at the school for five years, from 1911 through 1916.

Orwell's parents seem to have been less well-to-do than the parents of most of the other students at Crossgates. Orwell relates in his essay that by indirect means he gradually came to realize that Mr. and Mrs. Simpson, the school's Headmaster and Headmistress, had accepted Eric, as he was then called, as a sort of investment, at reduced tuition and boarding fees. However, as he saw the case, they did this not out of concern for his welfare, but rather because they thought he was bright and expected that with proper instruction he would win valuable scholarships to some of the great public schools, such as Eton, Winchester, or Wellington. This achievement would in turn help to add luster to the school's name and, as it was a private institution run in some measure for profit, attract wealthier students. The boy did not disappoint the Headmaster and Headmistress in this respect, because he won scholarships both to Eton (which he ultimately attended) and to Wellington.

Despite his success at school, the child detested the experience. From his own account, much of his experiences left him psychologically scarred. Beatings were commonplace. He recounts in the essay that soon after he arrived, at age eight, he was beaten by the Headmaster for wetting his bed. He initially made light of the beating, though it was with a bone-handled riding crop. But when the Headmaster overheard him tell his fellow students outside the room that "It didn't hurt," he was immediately beaten again. This time the Headmaster used such force that he broke the handle of the riding crop. The child had been beaten to the point that he collapsed "into a chair, weakly sniveling."

FEELINGS OF INFERIORITY

This beating marked the start of an educational process which instilled in the child an awful conviction of worthlessness, guilt, and weakness, which by his own account, he was not able to overcome for years. What he especially resented was the favoritism which he believed he saw in the treatment meted out by the Headmaster: the boys whose parents were wealthy and titled were treated with much more consideration than were the poorer boys who were attending the school at reduced tuition rates. "This was," he wrote in "Such, Such Were the Joys . . .," "the great abiding lesson of my boyhood: that I was in a world where it was not possible for me to be good . . . it brought home to me for the first time the harshness of the environment into which I had been flung." He did not add that his experiences at Crossgates also intensified his preoccupation with the effect of prolonged punishment on the human spirit, the relative importance of heredity and environment, the possibility of brainwashing, and the oppression of the defenseless. All these concerns are key themes in his writing.

In fairness to the proprietors of Crossgates, it must be said that Orwell's view of the school and the influence it was to have on his life was highly subjective. Christopher Hollis, Orwell's friend and the author of a biographical-critical study of him, refers to the Crossgates episode in more balanced terms. But the important point is not the objective reality of the school, but the effect which it had on Orwell during a key phase in his development. He had a sense of inferiority and failure which haunted him. In a world made for the strong, he was convinced that he was doomed to fail because school had convinced him that "success was measured not by what you did but by what you were." Even after he had won his two excellent scholarships, he felt that the school rejected him. He was in poor health, plagued by serious lung problems. But beyond any physical deficiencies, was the awful sense of failure and of the importance of class and birth. "In a world where the prime necessities were money, titled relatives, athleticism, tailor-made clothes, neatly brushed hair, a charming smile, I was no good," he wrote when he left Crossgates.

ETON

In 1917, when Orwell was fourteen years old, he matriculated at Eton. He became an idler where his studies were concerned. After the years of cramming in Latin and Greek, he did only enough at Eton to retain his scholarship—and no more. But he read widely, and even at this point impressed those around him as being an intellectual. To Cyril Connolly, one of his acquaintances at Eton, he proved by the force of his example "that there existed an alternative to character, Intelligence." His reading included George Bernard Shaw, Samuel Butler, and other great questioners of Victorian life. Their example helped Orwell learn to ask the hard questions about society.

While Orwell said that he was not well liked by the other boys at Eton, in part because of his poverty, this does not seem to be true. Christopher Hollis, two years ahead of him at Eton and therefore roughly his contemporary in the school, says that Orwell was regarded as something of a leader of the other boys, and also that in an environment in which beatings were a part of the system, he was in fact beaten rather less than the others. But Orwell's final judgment on Eton, published in an article in the *Observer,* "For Ever Eton," on August 1, 1948, described the school as offering "a tolerant and civilized atmosphere which gives each boy a fair chance of developing his individuality."

Orwell graduated from Eton at age eighteen and surprisingly decided to spend the next five years (1922-27) in Burma as an officer of the Indian Imperial Police. For a young man graduating from a top school like Eton, the normal next step would have been earning a University degree from Oxford or Cambridge. And apparently Orwell could have attended a university on a scholarship. Though the circumstances are somewhat obscure, Orwell, according to Christopher Hollis, was persuaded by one of his teachers at Eton that he ought to bypass the university route. "You've had enough of education. Take a job abroad and see something of the world," his teacher allegedly told him, and though Orwell was to regret this decision later, he went to Burma.

BURMA YEARS

Apparently he was a good officer, but he became increasingly disillusioned with his job and ceased to believe in the beneficial effects of imperialism. As he said in his essay "Marrakech," he came to believe that Europeans were fooling the people under colonial domination. He developed a tremendous amount of guilt at his supposedly privileged position. His experience in Burma is perhaps best illustrated in the famous essay "Shooting an Elephant," written a number of years after the fact, in which his performance of his duty as a police officer in Moulmein, Lower Burma, becomes the occasion for a graphic comment on what he saw as the essential self-imprisonment of all who served the cause of the British Government in its imperial domains.

A WRITING CAREER IS LAUNCHED

Feeling stifled by his job, Orwell came home on leave in 1927 and resigned from the service. Out of his Burmese experience came the novel *Burmese Days*, published in 1934. As is the case in every Orwell novel, there is one character in *Burmese Days* who has many of the qualities of Orwell himself. Here, the character is named Flory. He is also a civil servant in the British Raj in Burma who deteriorates under the influence of the system. But Orwell left the service, while Flory stayed in it until it indirectly brought about his death.

From 1927 until 1933 Orwell led a life of great poverty and deprivation. In 1933, he published *Down and Out in Paris and London*, a most graphic and subjective study of poverty and its effect upon the human spirit, and certainly one of the most truthful books on the subject that has ever been written.

At this time, Orwell also adopted his penname. "George" is a traditional English name; the patron Saint of England is St. George. "Orwell" is the name of a small river in Suffolk, by which he once lived. Why the name change? Some have theorized that Orwell had such a strong feeling of guilt over the class privilege from which he had benefited, first at Eton and then in Burma, that he turned his back on his social class by changing his name and living in poverty for nearly six years.

Orwell averaged about a book a year until World War II and his declining health made this rate of literary production impossible. Poverty was his subject in his next two novels, *A Clergyman's Daughter* (1935), and *Keep the Aspidistra Flying* (1936). The first book concerns the physical and spiritual impoverishment of moneyless middle-class genteel life in an English vicarage and in a dreadful girls' private school. The second novel is an even more powerful work about a conflict between Bohemianism and middle-class respectability which at least affirms the continuance of life.

By 1936, Orwell was earning enough from writing to live in the country. In 1936 he began a survey of unemployment in England and its effects. This resulted in 1937 in *The Road to Wigan Pier.* The Left Book Club, which had commissioned the book, published it and simultaneously disclaimed responsibility for its views. In the book, Orwell spoke of socialism as a possible remedy for the conditions which he had described.

That same year, Orwell married Eileen O'Shaughnessy. The marriage seems to have been a happy one. Orwell and his wife went to Spain, where the Spanish Civil War had broken out in that year. Orwell wished to study the Civil War and had received a publisher's advance to write a book about it. Quite characteristically, he decided that the best way to study the war was to fight in it. He became a member of the POUM (Partido Obrero de Unificacion Marxista, translated as Workers' Party of Marxist Unification). This was a radical Socialist-Trotskyite militia force which was opposed to the Communist-Stalinists of the International Brigades. The two factions ended up fighting each other as bitterly as they were to fight the Fascist forces of General Francisco Franco. The POUM was ruthlessly suppressed by Stalin's agents and their collaborators. Many Spanish members who had joined the POUM were arrested and executed. Orwell was badly wounded in the throat in fighting on the front lines. He was under such suspicion as a member of the POUM that he and his wife were lucky to escape from Spain alive. This experience acquainted him at firsthand with the nature of totalitarianism.

Out of this period came Orwell's book about his experience in Spain, *Homage to Catalonia* (1938). Orwell regarded the actions of the Communists in Spain as a betrayal of the popular revolution which might otherwise have given the working classes real freedom and status. A year later, Orwell published *Coming Up for Air*, a combination of nostalgia for pre-World War I times and conservative England, and apprehension at the appearance of "the streamlined men from Eastern Europe, who thought in slogans and spoke in bullets." With the outbreak of World War II, Orwell devoted himself to supporting the war effort and serving as a sergeant in the Home Guard in England. He had been rejected for military service because of his impaired health. He broadcast and wrote for the BBC, and also wrote many essays that praised England when compared with the totalitarian regimes of Hitler, Mussolini, and Stalin. As a result of his Spanish experience, Orwell was less deceived than most about Stalin's objectives in allowing Russia's entry into the war in 1941. And even in the fever of war hysteria, Orwell spoke out for reason and for facing the facts about the Germans.

Animal Farm, which would make Orwell world-famous, was written between November, 1943, and February, 1944. For some time Orwell was unable to find a publisher for it. This was due in part to the wartime paper scarcity, but it was also because Russia was England's ally. People realized that *Animal Farm* was a satire on the rise of totalitarian government in Russia under Lenin, Trotsky, and Stalin. *Animal Farm* finally appeared in August, 1945, when the Western Allies were becoming disenchanted with the Stalin regime. The same year, Orwell's beloved wife died. He attributed her death to lowered physical resistance due to the war, since both she and Orwell had consistently given up a part of their wartime food rations to feed children.

Orwell wrote his next great novel, *1984*, in the chaotic post-war period. But Orwell's health was shattered. He had a few months of happiness in 1949 when in the early summer he married Sonia Brownell, who assisted him in taking care of his adopted son. On January 21, 1950, as he was about to leave for a sanitarium in Switzerland, he had a tubercular hemorrhage and died.

SYNOPSIS

Sensing that his death is near, old Major, the prize boar of Manor Farm, shares with the other animals his dream of a new life. Old Major envisions a time when animals will rule themselves, free from the oppressive yoke of the true enemy: man. Old Major encourages the other animals to rebel against Mr. Jones, the owner of Manor Farm. When the opportunity arises, the animals drive Jones and his men from the farm, rename it "Animal Farm," and take over its operation. As the most clever animals, the pigs assume the day-to-day tasks of running the farm. They call old Major's theory "Animalism." On the barn wall, the pigs write the Seven Commandments of Animalism, which forbid animals to associate with human beings or to adopt human habits. Here are the Seven Commandments:

1. Whatever goes on two legs is an enemy.
2. Whatever goes upon four legs, or has wings, is a friend.
3. No animal shall wear clothes.
4. No animal shall sleep in a bed.
5. No animal shall drink alcohol.
6. No animal shall kill any other animal.
7. All animals are equal.

The leadership of the farm quickly falls to the two most ambitious and ruthless boars: Napoleon and Snowball. Although they compete with increasing bitterness for leadership of the farm, they nonetheless work together to beat off Jones when he attempts to recapture the farm. Snowball shows special bravery during the fight, which the animals rename the Battle of the Cowshed.

After this battle, the rivalry between Snowball and Napoleon deepens, especially over Snowball's idea for building a windmill which will bring the animals a better life. Napoleon opposes the idea and has his rival chased from the farm by his bodyguard of specially trained fierce dogs. Napoleon then takes over the windmill project himself, assuming full credit for the idea.

With the brutal work on the windmill and the increasing appetites of the nonproductive pigs and dogs, the living conditions of the other animals worsen. Napoleon uses Snowball as the scapegoat for everything that goes wrong on the farm. However, Squealer, a pig who is especially clever with words, manages to convince nearly all the animals that they are better off than before. Throughout, the strong workhorse Boxer works harder and harder to make the revolution a success. He meets every setback with the brave words "I will work harder"—and he does.

One by one, the Seven Commandments are rewritten to justify the pigs' actions, such as selling produce and eggs to humans and adopting human comforts. Whenever the animals complain, the threat of Jones's return is used to silence them. Boxer continues to work with all his strength.

When the partially-completed windmill collapses in a storm, the pigs blame Snowball and announce a project to rebuild it. To suppress increasing discontent, Napoleon purges the farm of malcontents: several pigs and other animals are executed. All the victims confess to being agents of Snowball.

Napoleon becomes an almost godlike, legendary figure: he is called "Leader" and appears in public only occasionally. He starts negotiations with the human owners of adjacent farms, Frederick and Pilkington, for the sale of some lumber. Although Napoleon appears to discredit Frederick and favor Pilkington, he ultimately sells the timber to the former. Right after this sale, Frederick attacks the farm and blows up the completed windmill. To rub salt in the wound, it is revealed that Frederick paid for the lumber with counterfeit bills.

Meanwhile, Boxer has exhausted the last of his strength and collapses. Although all the animals have been promised a gracious retirement, none has actually been rewarded with a pension. The animals are told that Boxer will be taken to the veterinarian; in reality, he is taken off to the knacker and sold for glue.

Although the animals rebuild the windmill and prosperity comes to the farm, only the pigs benefit. They become more human day by day. By the end of the book, they are drinking alcohol, walking on their hind legs, and carrying whips. Only one commandment—much altered—remains: "All animals are equal, but some animals are more equal than others."

Through the windows of the farmhouse, the brutally-treated work animals see Napoleon entertaining his human neighbors. It is impossible to tell the pigs from the men.

INTRODUCTION

Animal Farm may be read on several levels.

1. First, it is a simple animal fable. On the title page, Orwell himself called *Animal Farm* "a fairy story."

2. The novel can also be seen as a history of the development of Communist theory under Lenin and Stalin.

3. At the deepest level, *Animal Farm* is an account of how revolutions are made and subsequently corrupted, of the way people form political societies and exercise power in those societies. Finally, it is an illustration of the famous dictum on the nineteenth-century British historian, Lord Acton: "Power corrupts, and absolute power corrupts absolutely." Let's look at each of these interpretations more closely.

ANIMAL FARM AS A FABLE

Animal Farm represents a radical departure from the documentaries, essays, and novels that Orwell wrote in the 1930s; however, many commentators have noted that Orwell was well aware that the genre of the beast fable was uniquely suited to his own purposes of social and political satire in this novel. Traditionally in such fables, each animal represents not only itself—and in the finest examples of the genre such as *Animal Farm* the animal characters are always recognizable as animals—but also a single aspect of human nature which the author has fixed upon for comment. The conventions of the animal fable enabled Orwell to examine simply and directly the horrifying moral decisions made within the Soviet political system. In *Animal Farm,* Orwell keeps the reader conscious simultaneously of the human traits satirized and of the animals as animals.

In addition, fairy tales take place in a world where people suffer or succeed for reasons beyond their control. People might live simply because they are beautiful—or die because they are not. Fairy tales do not moralize or criticize; rather, they are visions of a highly simplified version of life. This is what Orwell presents in *Animal Farm.*

Finally, the term "fable" is also a story which was once believed but which has since turned out to be untrue. *Animal Farm* is thus a fable of Communist revolutionary ideology. Part of its structure involves a movement by certain of the animals on the farm away from what they believed to be objectively true (Marxist ideology, on which the Russian Revolution was based), toward the death of belief in such ideology, and finally its replacement by a sham used to keep the less intelligent members of the community from finding out the truth.

ANIMAL FARM AS THE DEVELOPMENT OF COMMUNISM AND A HISTORY OF RUSSIA

In 1947, just as *Animal Farm* had made him famous, Orwell published an essay entitled "Why I Write." "Every line of serious work that I have written since 1936," Orwell wrote, "has been written, directly or indirectly, against totalitarianism and for democratic socialism, as I understand it. It seems to me nonsense, in a period like our own, to think that one can avoid writing of such subjects. Everyone writes of them in one guise or another. It is simply a question of which side one takes and what approach one follows."

Animal Farm is a satire, using the device of the animal fable. As such, each of the animals is used to represent a particular aspect of Communism in the former Soviet Union.

Old Major represents Karl Marx; old Major's ideas on the oppression of animals by human beings is Marxist doctrine. The men stand for Marx's capitalists, while the animals are the working men and women. Major can also be seen as Lenin, before the Revolution. Mr. Jones is Czar Nicholas II, overthrown by the Communists. The animals' actual revolution is the Russian Revolution of 1917. Napoleon is Stalin, and Snowball is Trotsky. Squealer is Stalin's propaganda agent.

Pilkington and Foxwood Farm stand for Great Britain, while Frederick and Pinchfield Farm stand for Germany. Orwell parallels Russia's relationship to these countries in Napoleon's dealings with them. The Battle of the Cowshed, the first invasion of Animal Farm, is the anti-revolutionary invasion of the new Soviet Russia by the West; the Battle of the Windmill, the second invasion, represents the German invasion of Russia during World War II.

The repeated attempts to build the windmill refer to Stalin's Five-Year Plans. The horrifying repression of Stalin's rule is shown in the gradual enslavement of the animals, his purges, trials, and phony confessions. Finally, the Teheran Conference in alluded to in the novel's last scene. Napoleon sitting down with the men at the drunken party parallels Stalin's meeting with representatives from the West.

Moses, the raven, symbolizes organized religion. Napoleon and the pigs let Moses stay because they think that religion will dull the other animals to their pain. This is Karl Marx's argument that religion is the "opiate of the masses." Moses is helpful to the pigs as long as he does not get in the way of Napoleon's plans for the animals.

In addition, *Animal Farm* provides a history of Russia. It includes Russia's foreign relations from the October Revolution (1917) to the uneasy relationship between Russia and the Western democracies as the Second World War drew to its close (1944–45).

ANIMAL FARM AS AN ACCOUNT OF POWER AND CORRUPTION

In the same essay, Orwell wrote: "*Animal Farm* was the first book in which I tried, with full consciousness of what I was doing, to fuse political purpose and artistic purpose into one whole . . . . Looking back through my work, I see that it is invariably where I lacked a political purpose that I wrote lifeless books and was betrayed into purple passages, sentences without meaning, decorative adjectives, and humbug generally."

Orwell was writing about a political system which had begun full of promise and which had deteriorated into tyranny. One of his purposes in using the figures of beasts to portray the actions of men was to imply that men in their political communities were often no better than beasts. In the last line of *Animal Farm,* when the animals, having taken possession of the Farm are imitating the ways of men, Orwell comments dryly: "it was impossible to say which was which."

ANIMAL FARM

CHAPTER ONE

Readers are introduced to the deteriorating situation on Manor Farm. Mr. Jones, the farm's owner, has lost control of his animals and property. He falls asleep one night so drunk that he cannot even remember to shut and lock the animals into their barn and cages. With Jones out of the way for the night, the animals of the Farm come to a secret meeting, called by old Major, a majestic-looking pig. He wishes to communicate a strange dream to the other animals. At the meeting, old Major gives a spellbinding oration about the oppressed condition of the animals and introduces them to a new and stirring revolutionary song, "Beasts of England." The animals are so delighted with the song that they make a tremendous uproar as they sing it, whereupon Jones is awakened from his drunken sleep and scatters the animals by firing a shotgun into the night. Jones thinks that a fox is in the yard, but he does not suspect that the beasts are plotting a revolt.

COMMENT

Old Major, the majestic old boar, represents Karl Marx (1818-1883), the prime theoretician of Marxism, which became Communism. Old Major's dream (Marx's dream) is the proletarian revolution. Marx stated it most succinctly in *The Communist Manifesto* (1848), which he wrote in collaboration with Friedrich Engels. The first line reads: "The history of all hitherto existing society is the history of class struggles." This is the thesis of Major's impassioned speech late at night in the barn of Mr. Jones's farm as he exhorts the animals to throw off the chains which bind them.

Old Major says, "There, comrades, is the answer to all our problems. It is summed up in a single word—Man." Old Major believes that Man is the only enemy that the animals have. The boar preaches that if the animals remove man from the scene, the root cause of hunger and overwork will be abolished forever. Old Major's maxims become the principles by which the animals build their utopia—and by which they are subsequently undone. In large part, this is because old Major's view of human nature is grossly oversimplified. As a result, an entire society comes to be established on the belief that man is the sole cause of animals' misery, their only evil. Such a simplistic belief can easily be manipulated for selfish ends in the same way as the animals' unrealistic view of human nature.

Old Major's speech stirs the other animals, most of whom are not nearly as bright as the prize Middle White boar. Old Major uses exactly the arguments which would appeal to his audience: the soil of England is fertile, there should be enough for everyone, but in all England not a single animal is free, and everywhere Man robs the animals of their just compensation for labor. All this is accepted uncritically. Major had said that he would relate a wonderful dream that he had experienced—but once he has an audience, he stirs it with a rousing speech first and delays the retelling of the dream until the end, for good reason.

Old Major's speech is a burlesque version of the Marxist theories of class struggle, the labor theory of value, and surplus value, as well as the idea that the animals, who alone are productive (as are the workers, peasants, and intellectuals in Marxist theory), should regard Man, "the only creature that consumes without producing" (the class of the bourgeoisie and the capitalists according to Marx and Lenin), as their enemy and should, in keeping with their duty of enmity toward Man, revolt against his domination.

Of course, this is a fantasy; the animals are too ignorant to see that Major is cleverly playing with them. But

Orwell, in a master stroke of satire, implies that old Major, at least, is probably sincere. He utters a number of Commandments in his speech, as though he were a primal lawgiver; these will be embodied later into a sort of law for Animal Farm. They will also be rewritten as all principles of all revolutions undergo such changes for the worse, once the revolutionary spirit is corrupted by knavish leaders who seek only their own ends. "Even when you have conquered Man," says old Major, "do not adopt his vices." In his simplistic view of the world, animals must consider themselves entirely good and Man as entirely evil. "All animals are equal," old Major says, after he brings the animals to a vote on whether the rats should be considered comrades also. The vote is in the affirmative.

Finally, old Major leads the animals in singing "Beasts of England," which can be seen as a burlesque on the Communist Internationale: "Arise, ye prisoners of starvation! Arise, ye slaves, no more in thrall. . . !"

But old Major is not only the theoretician, he is the moving force of the Revolution on the farm. Major is thus not only Marx, he is also Lenin, who not only sees the Revolution into being but also rules Russia afterward. Lenin died at age fifty-three and left others to the task of completing the work of the revolutionary government; old Major dies in his sleep three days after his speech.

Historically, of course, Chapter One corresponds to the period before and during World War I, where Tsarism in Russia was finally collapsing. The Tsar, like Mr. Jones, was incompetent, and thus power passed into stronger hands. But as we consider the satire in Chapter One, it would be well to keep in mind Orwell's presentation of Major as sincere in his beliefs—for it is difficult to make a revolution without initial sincerity on the part of the leaders. Old Major is subtle and devious in his appeal to the animals. But he is sincere in his belief that the animals are good and deserve the fruits of their own labor, while people are evil and rob the animals of what is rightfully theirs. Mr. Jones (the Tsar), being absorbed only in gross pleasures and forgetful of the duties imposed on him, must be replaced. But who will replace him?

As the chapter ends, where there has been torpid calm there is now great unrest.

CHAPTER TWO

With the exception of Moses, the tame raven, all of the animals had attended the meeting in the barn and heard old Major's speech. The animals are enthusiastic about the Revolution-to-be. Since they are not as subtle or as intelligent as old Major, the animals cannot perceive the fallacies of the speech. But they prepare for the revolt, for even the dullest creature is no longer content with life on Manor Farm.

The pigs, led by Snowball and Napoleon and a smaller pig named Squealer, expand old Major's teachings into a complete code of behavior. They include a system for the regulation of thought and "animal discipline." To this system they have given the name of "Animalism."

The Revolution, when it comes, takes the animals by surprise. It is a spontaneous rising fostered by Mr. Jones's incompetence. He had been a good farmer, but was despondent because he had lost money in a lawsuit. Instead of taking action, Mr. Jones had spent his time feeding the raven Moses on crusts of bread soaked in beer. The Revolution is precipitated by Mr. Jones's getting so drunk one weekend that he forgets to feed the animals or milk the cows. Without any planning, the animals break into the feed bins and help themselves, for they will starve if they do not do something. Rapidly they seize Manor Farm and drive out Jones, his wife, and the hired hands. The animals smash up everything which reminds them of the former human owners of the Farm. Then they paint on a wall the Seven Commandments of Animalism. These commandments had been formulated by the pigs as an "unalterable law" for the guidance of all on the Farm. Finally they change the name of the place from Manor Farm to Animal Farm and march off to the harvest, eager to work for themselves rather than for Mr. Jones.

COMMENT

In Orwell's satire, Animalism represents Marxism. The Seven Commandments of Animalism, formulated by Snowball and Napoleon, come from the old Major's speech. These Commandments are a form of propaganda. They are designed to spark national pride and encourage a sense of cooperation and exclusiveness. The Commandments are:

1. Whatever goes upon two legs is an enemy.
2. Whatever goes upon four legs, or has wings, is a friend.
3. No animal shall wear clothes.
4. No animal shall sleep in a bed.
5. No animal shall drink alcohol.
6. No animal shall kill any other animal.
7. All animals are equal.

This is the philosophy of the Revolution. It is important to keep these Commandments in mind as a standard by which the progress of the Animal Farm experiment may be judged. In terms of Orwell's satiric purpose, the corruption of the Revolution from "plain living and high thinking" to more self-seeking ends on the part of some takes place in the very moment Jones is thrown off the Farm. The cows are lowing even as Jones is evicted; nobody has milked them for twenty-four hours. The pigs oblige by milking them, as the pigs have found that their trotters are adaptable to such human tasks as climbing ladders or milking cows, though with some initial awkwardness. Pails of milk, five in all, are the result, and the other animals look hungrily at them. "What is going to happen to all that milk?" asks one of the animals. But Napoleon exhorts them to pay no attention to the milk but to go forward with Comrade Snowball to begin the harvest in the hayfield. When the animals return from the hayfield in the evening, they notice that the milk has disappeared. This is the first of many such unexplained events. Obviously, the pigs have disposed of the milk, either selling it or drinking it themselves. For while all animals are equal, the pigs already believe that they are superior.

For Orwell, this incident is indicative of his central thesis, the abuse of power. Orwell suggests that there will always be some group to pervert such an idealistic Revolution to its own advantage. Here, he uses the incident of the pigs and the milk to drive home his point.

The Seven Commandments of Animalism have the status of revealed and unchanging law, spoken by the semidivine prophet old Major. The boar wished that the animals should not be corrupted by contact with humans.

Moses, the tame raven, has told the animals of a shadowy never-never land called Sugarcandy Mountain, to which animals go when they die. Moses represents organized religion; Sugarcandy Mountain represents heaven. The pigs tolerate—and even encourage—Moses because he placates the animals and helps them endure great hardships. Marx called religion "the opiate of the masses."

Mollie, a white mare, still hopes to be able to wear ribbons. Snowball cautions her after the Revolution that ribbons are the mark of human beings—they are clothing, and no animal shall wear clothes. She discards the ribbon—but is not really convinced. Ultimately Mollie will desert the animal cause and return to the society of humans, voluntarily working for them. She might be characterized as either a "right-deviationist" (one who in Communist theory veers away from "Socialist" principles in the direction of capitalism), or as a "reactionary" who subverts the Revolution.

Orwell's historical satire, especially regarding the history of Russia subsequent to the 1917 Revolution, is open to varying interpretations. Here are several books you will find useful for further study. The first is *Three Who Made a Revolution*, by Bertram D. Wolfe (1948). This is a biographical history of Lenin, Trotsky, and Stalin. The second is the well-known *To the Finland Station*, by Edmund Wilson. First published in 1940, this book studies not only the Russian Revolution and Lenin's part in it, but also the entire European tradition of revolutionary socialism. Finally, you may wish to consult Louis Fischer's biographies of Lenin and Stalin. Fisher's *The Life of Lenin* (1964) is especially interesting if you wish to learn more about the period and the people who are Orwell's concern in *Animal Farm*.

CHAPTER THREE

This chapter describes the enormous amount of work that must be done on Animal Farm. The animals, especially the horses, throw themselves into the work unreservedly. Although there are apparently no social classes on Animal Farm, the pigs seem aloof from the others. Instead of actually working, they "directed and supervised the others." They are the self-appointed leaders in a society of "comrades."

At first, the pigs' cleverness is useful because they can think of a way around every difficulty. Orwell doesn't specify whether they are really more clever by nature, or whether they simply take upon themselves the mastery of difficult intellectual tasks. There is initially a high level of morality on Animal Farm, as all temptation to steal has ostensibly been done away with by the Revolution. With the human beings gone, there is at first more to eat. Boxer the horse has tremendously strong muscles and is a tireless and dedicated worker. Unfortunately, he does not have much ability to analyze what he is doing. His answer to every problem is his personal motto: "I will work harder!" The pigs are glad to take this over and make it into a slogan.

There are a few animals on the fringes who seem less than ideally happy—the cat, for instance, who has a habit of vanishing at peculiar intervals. Old Benjamin, the donkey, is also less than enthusiastic about the revolution. The donkey does his work exactly as he had done it under Mr. Jones, never volunteering for more and never doing less. But he is careful to offer no opinions on the Revolution. The cat, however, outdoes him in this, for when a vote was taken, the cat was found to have voted on both sides of the issue.

The pigs arrange a ceremony to take the place of Sunday religious worship. It includes the hoisting of a Flag of the Animals, a hoof and horn in white painted on an old green tablecloth.

There are debates over policy, but somehow the pigs always seem to control the outcome. While Snowball and Napoleon are the most active in the debates, it becomes apparent that they rarely agree. Meanwhile educational programs and Committees have been organized. In addition, the pigs have attempted to have all the animals memorize the Seven Principles of Animalism. Since many are not capable of such an intellectual feat, Snowball declares that the Seven Commandments can be reduced to a single maxim: "Four Legs Good, Two Legs Bad." The sheep like this maxim so much that they spend hours bleating it over and over.

At the end of the chapter, it is evident that there is strain between Napoleon and Snowball over ideology and the exercise of power.

COMMENT

Orwell hoped for a Revolution that would convert world inequality into justice and true fraternity. At the same time, he saw how the motto of the French Revolution— "Liberty, Equality, Fraternity"—had been perverted. In this chapter, we can already see Napoleon at work seizing power for himself, undercutting his chief rival, and setting himself on a path which will result in the same kind of autocracy which Animal Farm had experienced under Jones.

For example, after Mr. Jones's expulsion from the farm, the animals finally gather the courage to enter the farmhouse. They tiptoe from room to room, afraid to speak above a whisper and gazing with a kind of awe at the unbelievable luxury, at the beds with their feather mattresses, the mirrors, the plush sofa, the Brussels carpet, the lithography of Queen Victoria over the drawing-room mantelpiece.

To the animals, the farmhouse represents all the evil that is humanity. It has beds and whiskey and many of the other things that old Major has encouraged his followers to shun. It becomes significant later, then, that the pigs move into the farmhouse. It is an early sign that they are assuming the role of the oppressor, Mr. Jones.

Further, there are basic differences between Snowball and Napoleon. Snowball is a great organizer, like the figure he was modeled on—Leon Trotsky. Napoleon is a ruthless, cruel leader, like the figure he was modeled on—Josef Stalin. Like Trotsky, Snowball forms many Committees, such as the Wild Comrades' Re-Education Committee and the Whiter Wool Movement. Snowball also organizes literacy classes, which are a great success, for by autumn most of the animals are literate to some degree. The hard-working Boxer is never able to learn the alphabet beyond the first four letters. Because he performs enormous work and is completely under the direction of the pigs, he is one of the most valuable members of the community, even though he cannot learn how to read and write. He symbolizes workers who follow totalitarian systems blindly and sincerely, believing that the system would be their salvation.

Napoleon, in contrast, is utterly ruthless. He takes litters of puppies from Jessie and Bluebell, and makes himself responsible for their education. Through intensive training and conditioning, he will turn the dogs into a weapon he can use against the other animals. These fierce, specially-trained dogs correspond to the Secret Police which Stalin used to repress the population.

The Revolution initially improves the lot of the animals on the Farm; after all, things could hardly have been worse than they were when Mr. Jones was the ruler. This reinforces Orwell's satire: Russia under Tsarism had finally ground to a halt under the extraordinary stresses of the First World War. Under the impetus of the new order on the Farm, with the animals' belief that they are now working for themselves rather than for a human exploiter, life on the farm does improve, at least for a time. But how much of this improvement may be attributed to the Revolution, Orwell asks.

Squealer the pig represents the totalitarian propaganda agencies that manipulated the workers in the USSR. When the animals grumble over the pigs getting the farm's milk, Squealer is the one who invents plausible reasons for such an unequal sharing of the Farm's resources. "We pigs are brainworkers," he tells the others, and assures them that it is for the sake of everyone that the pigs are to be fed better. If the pigs fail in their duty, he warns, the hated Farmer Jones might come back. "Surely, comrades," says Squealer, "there is no one among you who wants to see Jones come back?"

The technique of proving, or attempting to prove, a point by phrasing it as a question was much used as a rhetorical device by Stalin, as may be seen from his writings and speeches. "What is Leninism?" Stalin had asked, rhetorically, in his book *Foundations of Leninism*.

As the end of the chapter, readers can see that Snowball and Napoleon, who should be working together in the leadership of the Farm which they have assumed, are actually working at cross purposes. For example, Orwell says, "Snowball and Napoleon were by far the most active in the debates. But it was noticed that these two were never in agreement: whatever suggestion either of them made, the other could be counted on to oppose it."

This comment shows how the two pigs struggle for

power. Partly, this is the struggle between Trotsky and Stalin after the death of Lenin. But more generally, this scene (and others like it that portray Snowball and Napoleon fighting for supremacy), is the struggle that occurs in any society in which the people at large have no effective say in their government.

This observation is reinforced in Snowball's simplification of the seven commandments into one slogan: "Four legs good, two legs bad." The sheep—who represent society's followers—are especially satisfied with this reduction of the doctrine and so chant the slogan at any opportunity. This is just the kind of slogan that is easy to understand, dangerously simplified, and flexible enough to manipulate for leaders such as Napoleon and Snowball who are determined to seize power. Something is bound to happen which will affect the Farm's future.

CHAPTER FOUR

The open break between Snowball and Napoleon is temporarily averted by an outside threat to the new order on Animal Farm. The animals have been spreading the news of their Revolution to the neighboring farms by means of pigeons, who have been persuading the neighboring animals to join the Revolution. The pigeons have also taught the animals the anthem "Beasts of England." Obviously the farmers whose estates border Animal Farm will not stand for this.

But the opposition is weak. Farmer Jones has spent much of his time sitting in a tavern drinking and complaining about how he had been thrown off his own farm. But his words initially carry little weight, for the other farmers do nothing. His two adjoining neighbors are Mr. Pilkington of Foxwood, an "easy-going gentleman farmer" and Mr. Frederick of Pinchfield, a "tough, shrewd man, perpetually involved in lawsuits." These two men are enemies, and this is lucky for the animals of the Farm, because it prevents a united front.

At first, the two neighbors of Animal Farm are too busy with their own quarrel to pay much attention to what is going on at Animal Farm. They laugh at the animals' experiment. But when they see that the animals on the Farm seem to be flourishing, and when their own herds and flocks give evidence of rebellion and have learned "Beasts of England," the men finally conclude that they must take action. Only their bickering and inefficiency have saved Animal Farm so far.

One day a flock of pigeons comes to Animal Farm and warns the animals that Jones and all of his men, with reinforcements from both Foxwood and Pinchfield, are on their way to the Farm. The animals have time to make preparations. Snowball, having read an old book on the campaigns of Julius Caesar, has organized a defense. As a result, there is a fierce engagement but the humans are driven off. They make an ignominious retreat.

The animals have a ceremony celebrating the victory. They confer a brass medal and the title "Animal Hero, First Class," on those who had done the most for the victory: Snowball and Boxer. There is also a posthumous award of "Animal Hero, Second Class," on the sheep who had been killed by the men. This confrontation comes to be known as the Battle of the Cowshed, and holidays are established on the Farm to commemorate it.

COMMENT

It reinforces Orwell's satire to have a number symbols in the novel. We see many here. The farmers whose homes border Animal Farm symbolize the fear of Bolshevism in other countries after the 1917 Revolution in Russia. Pilkington symbolized England; Frederick represents the Kaiser's Germany. Their quarrel symbolizes the First World War. The Battle of the Cowshed corresponds to the various attacks of both internal and external enemies on the new Soviet regime. On March 3, 1918, Germany and other countries of the Central Powers in the First World War were battling Russia, and the Germans were at the point of taking Petrograd (now Leningrad). This would have inflicted a crushing blow to the hopes of the Bolshevik government. At this point, Russia signed the Treaty of Brest-Litovsk with Germany. Thus Lenin and his associates settled temporarily with one of their enemies, though at a very high cost because the Germans insisted on very severe terms in this treaty.

These events are reduced to an absurdity by Orwell in the Battle of the Cowshed through the mock-epic. Among great satiric writers in English, Swift, Pope, and Fielding have used this form. See, for example, Fielding's *Tom Jones,* Book IV, Chapter 8, for a "mock-battle in the Homeric style."

In this chapter, the enemies of the Revolution are shown to be incompetent, and at this point not superior ethically to the adherents of the Revolution, most of whom are still sincerely dedicated to its principles. Because the animals are still united in their support of the Revolution while their enemies are divided, the animals win. Their victory reinforces their morale.

CHAPTER FIVE

Mollie, the mare, begins to act in an odd manner, and soon Clover finds occasion to speak to her on the basis of "comradely advice." Clover has seen Mollie allowing one of Mr. Pilkington's men to talk to her and stroke her nose, but Mollie denies this and gallops away. Investigating further, Clover goes to Mollie's stall and finds a pile of lump sugar and several bunches of ribbons. There can be little doubt that Mollie has become an "enemy of the people." Soon after, Mollie disappears. Later she is seen, gaily adorned with a scarlet ribbon, pulling a cart in town. Mollie has placed herself outside the animal ranks. As a result, she is never again mentioned by her former associates.

Meanwhile, the Farm is falling on hard times after their victory over Mr. Jones and the other farmers. The weather becomes bitterly cold and it is impossible to farm. The animals hold many meetings and discussions, and it becomes clear that there is a split between Snowball and Napoleon on almost every issue. Snowball is the better speaker at meetings, and he sways the animals to his side by his brilliant persuasiveness. Napoleon says little but quietly builds up machinery for rallying support. The sheep are his loyal supporters; they often break into a chant of "Four legs good, two legs bad" at crucial points in Snowball's speeches.

The conflict comes to a head with a violent debate over the windmill, which causes the break between Napoleon and Snowball. Snowball had proposed the windmill as the solution to the Farm's problems; it could be harnessed to a dynamo to provide electric power and to run various labor-saving power machinery. The animals are shocked by these proposals, but Snowball is persuasive. Snowball works furiously on the plans for the machinery, but Napoleon says little except that the windmill will not work and is a waste of time.

All the animals take sides; there are bitter factional disputes. Only Benjamin, the skeptical donkey, refuses to take sides, saying that regardless of what happens life will go on as it always has in the past—badly. At a general meeting, Napoleon speaks against the plan and Snowball in favor of it. Snowball launches into a brilliant oration on behalf of the windmill. He seems to be having his way, when suddenly nine enormous dogs, with brass-studded heavy collars, bound into the barn upon Napoleon's whistle. They spring at Snowball, who just has time to run out the door and outrun the dogs. The other animals are too terrified to take action. Snowball disappears, and Napoleon announces that effective immediately the Sunday morning debates are cancelled. Animals will assemble on Sunday morning to salute the Animal Flag, to sing "Beasts of England," and to receive their orders for the week. There will not be any debate. Animals who don't like the new arrangement and who might have spoken out against it are growled at by Napoleon's dogs. These animals find it prudent not to say anything.

Squealer goes around the Farm to explain the reason for the change. In the spring, Napoleon announces that the windmill will be built, and while everyone is surprised at this evident reversal of his position, Napoleon has taken over Snowball's entire plan. Squealer lets it be known that Napoleon was not really opposed to the windmill; he had seemed to oppose it in order to get rid of the dangerous influence, Snowball.

COMMENT

Napoleon finally seizes the Revolution. Force and terrorism win out over Snowball's more rational approach. The fierce dogs represent Stalin's Secret Police. Readers can see this in the following passage: "In spite of the shock that Snowball's expulsion had given them, the animals were dismayed by this announcement."

After Snowball's expulsion, Napoleon quickly seizes the reigns of power. He announces that the Sunday-morning Meetings will come to an end. All questions relating to the working of the farm will be settled by a committee of pigs. The committee will meet in private and announce their decisions later. All debates have halted. The speed of Napoleon's seizure of power shows that a dictatorship has been established.

On one level, Orwell is alluding to Stalin's assumption of power in the Soviet Union. On another level, however, Orwell is using satire to show how people are deceived when someone is determined to manipulate them for his own purposes. The fact that the animals do not see how their future is being foreshadowed is one of the novel's most brutal ironies.

Leon Trotsky, the model for Snowball, was an organizer. He was invaluable in rallying the Red Army when the new regime was reeling under both invasion and civil turmoil after the Russian Revolution. Once Stalin had consolidated his power by the use of terrorism, forced-labor, and the secret police, Trotsky was forced out of the Party. He was exiled and assassinated in Mexico by Stalin's agent.

Boxer, the loyal but ignorant workhorse, adds to his slogan of "I will work harder!" a second slogan, "Napoleon is always right." If Napoleon has denounced Snowball, it must be so, says Boxer. With Snowball's expulsion, the skull of old Major had been disinterred and set up as a symbol. After the Animal Flag is raised on Sunday mornings, the animals are required to file past the skull in a reverent manner before entering the barn. This symbolizes the preservation of Lenin's body after his death in 1924 and his entombment in a glass coffin near the Kremlin. People filed by to look upon the founder of the Revolution.

The bitterly cold weather and impossiblity of farming represent Soviet crop failures and agricultural inefficiencies in the 1920s. This culminated in severe famine. The windmill symbolizes the Soviet New Economic Policy, the first Five-Year Plan, and the mechanization of agriculture.

CHAPTER SIX

The year after Snowball's exile, the animals work like slaves. In addition to a sixty-hour work week, Napoleon requires the animals to "volunteer" for work on Sundays. Although the animals are working harder than ever, the results are disappointing, as the harvest is less successful than in the previous year.

Further, the windmill presents great difficulties, although it was to have been the mainstay of the Farm's economic well-being. The animals have a very hard time breaking and transporting the limestone to the building site. The situation is partly saved by Boxer, who voluntarily works very long hours. Everyone admires his dedication. Boxer is careless of his own physical strength and health in the service of the Farm. Various materials vital to the Farm's operation appear if by magic: nails, iron for the horses' shoes, and the machinery for the windmill. The animals do not realize that the pigs are trading with the "outside"—which has been forbidden.

Napoleon has decided to trade with the neighboring farms, which he announces to the animals at a Sunday meeting. There is no discussion of his radical decision, even though it violates the Commandments, specifically the resolutions against the use of money or the engaging in trade with humans which the animals had passed at the time of the Revolution.

Napoleon employs a sly lawyer, Mr. Whymper, as an intermediary between the Farm and the humans. It is even rumored that Napoleon will enter into a business deal with one of his neighbors. Worse, the pigs move out of the sty and into the farmhouse. By the winter, there have been some upsetting changes in the ordering of the Farm. But the windmill, which is now half-finished, compensates for much of the disorder, and the animals are proud of it.

One morning after a raging storm in November, the animals awake to a terrible sight: the windmill is in ruins. Napoleon is at a loss for a moment; then he roars: "Snowball has done this thing!" He pronounces a death sentence in absentia upon Snowball, and offers a reward for his capture dead or alive. He ends by exhorting the animals to rebuild the windmill.

COMMENT

Like other symbols in the novel, the windmill is used to help create the satire and to serve as a means of conveying the novel's theme. For Snowball, the windmill was a sign of the enlightened progress upon which the community of Animal Farm was created. Snowball intended the windmill to bring great comfort to the animals' lives. To Napoleon, in contrast, the windmill was a means by which the animals can be kept busy. When the windmill is finally finished, Napoleon will use it to extend his power and his personal comfort. To the animals, the windmill is a barely comprehended symbol of a better life to which they all aspire—and that none will realize.

The windmill episode probably represents historically the failure of the first Russian Five-Year Plan and the equal failure of a modified economic system (The New Economic Policy, promulgated by Lenin in 1921). Further, it was in 1921 that Lenin, seeing that Russia would need to obtain certain essential materials from the outside world by trade, entered into negotiations with representatives of various foreign countries to establish trade relations. Under the stress of war and revolution, Russia's nationalized industries had seriously deteriorated. There was widespread famine. Departing temporarily from Marxist ideology, Russia began to enter into trade with outside capitalists.

Conditions on the Farm require modification of the former revolutionary principles. This modification comes about in a very sly manner, which the ordinary workers only dimly perceive because they have been too busy performing heavy physical labor.

After the pigs move into the house, the other animals remember that the Fourth Commandment is: "No animal shall sleep in a bed." Clover is especially curious. Unable to read the Commandments herself, Clover brings Muriel, who spells it out: "No animal shall sleep in a bed with sheets." Clover had not remembered that the Commandment said anything about sheets, but decides that it must be so if Muriel sees it in writing. At the same time Squealer arrives with some dogs to "explain" the matter. The pigs, he tells them, are brainworkers and therefore for the good of the Farm need the rest provided by the beds. The sheets, on the other hand, are a human invention and so are prohibited. Squealer "proves" that the pigs are justified in living in the house and in getting up an hour later than the others.

Here Orwell is probably thinking more of Nazi propaganda—of the Big Lie, the dictum put into practice by Hitler and by his sinister Propaganda Minister, Dr. Goebbels. They believed that if a lie were repeated often and emphatically enough it would be accepted as true. So Squealer convinces even the reluctant, with terror (the dogs) always at his side as a final "persuader."

The revision of the Commandments shows how the past is changed to make it conform to the present. To be in the position to rewrite history is to control both the past and the future. Throughout the story, the Commandments are revised, one by one, to rationalize what

Napoleon wants to do. Having only the side of the barn as a source for the Commandments, the animals are forced to accept the changes as they are mysteriously made. This symbolism culminates when the last commandment of Animalism is perverted: "All animals are equal, but some animals are more equal than others."

As the chapter ends, Napoleon has created a scapegoat, Snowball, for the shortcomings of his regime. Snowball, who had once been a hero among the animals, is now an exiled and hunted malefactor. This is what totalitarians must do to maintain power.

CHAPTER SEVEN

The Farm is very short on food and supplies that winter because of inefficiency and a defective production and distribution system. Napoleon plans to distract the animals from these problems by finding a scapegoat—Snowball. As a result, Napoleon defines Snowball as a traitor who has been in league at different times both with Mr. Pilkington and Mr. Frederick. Meanwhile Napoleon has a revolt on his hands. Napoleon had concealed the shortage of food from his human agent, Mr. Whymper, but he negotiates a contract to sell four hundred eggs a week to the "outside." This will keep the Farm going all winter. The hens revolt against the loss of their eggs, but Napoleon ruthlessly suppresses the rebellion. Calling together the animals, he says that there are traitors and agents of Snowball in their midst. To everyone's amazement, a number of animals denounce themselves and confess to a variety of crimes, whereupon they are immediately executed by the fierce dogs. Blood flows freely, and the survivors are both terrified and cowed. Some of them remember the Sixth Commandment: "No animal shall kill any other animal." But this seems to have been forgotten in practice if not in theory, under the need to exterminate the "saboteurs and traitors." As the chapter ends, Napoleon has prohibited even the singing of "Beasts of England," and has substituted instead a much more innocuous and unmelodic anthem composed by Minimus, the poet.

COMMENT

This chapter compresses and gives perspective to a period of nearly twenty years of Soviet-style Communist government. The period begins with the failure of the Soviet regime's economic policies in the 1920s and resulting famine. But the major part of this sequence of events has to do with the amazing series of Soviet purge trials of the 1930s.

Like any other successful dictator, Napoleon must remove any potential or real opposition. At the same time, he must prove his power to make other people suffer. Here, Napoleon does just that. Under the pretext of quelling rebellion, Napoleon makes four pigs "confess" and then executes them. The pigs claim to have been secretly in touch with Snowball ever since his expulsion, that they had worked with him to destroy the windmill, and that they had entered into an agreement with him to give Animal Farm to Mr. Frederick. These particular pigs are logical targets: they were the four pigs who had protested when Napoleon had abolished the Sunday meetings. Executing pigs—one of his "own"—is an inescapable reminder that no one is safe from the leader's grasp.

Napoleon's call for "truth" sets off a wave of hysterical confessions of guilt and immediate executions. This makes Napoleon's power both visible and immediate. The animals are horrified, but there is virtually nothing they can do. Napoleon is becoming more and more powerful. To reinforce his power, he appears only with due ceremony and then only surrounded by his bodyguard of fierce dogs. After all, a deity cannot mingle with his followers, or they will discover that he is not all-powerful.

The Soviet purges shocked the world for their brutality and irrationality, just as the purges shocked the farm animals. The purges were accompanied with famous "show trials" held in Moscow between August 1936 and March 1938. During the trials, a number of high-ranking Soviet leaders were accused of treacherous acts against the State, convicted, and nearly all executed. But the truly remarkable thing about the trials was the willingness of the defendants to confess. They were convicted almost entirely on the basis of their own unsupported confessions.

We see that a totalitarian state is not satisfied with simple obedience; rather, it must have loyalty so intense that even the condemned traitors will be their own accusers. Orwell showed naked lust for power, insane suspiciousness, and the blackest double-dealing at work. The abolition of "Beasts of England" signifies the death of the Revolution and its replacement by a police state.

CHAPTER EIGHT

After the terror inspired by the public confessions and executions dies down somewhat, several of the animals remembered, or thought they remembered, the wording of the Sixth Commandment: "No animal shall kill any other animal." This seems very clear even to the dullest mind, and it is further observed that the executions somehow violate this Commandment. Clover again asks Muriel to read her the Sixth Commandment. And Muriel reads: "No animal shall kill any other animal without cause."

The animals do not remember the additional two words, "without cause," but decide that since they are written they must be so. Since those who had been executed had given cause by being traitors, it followed that they were justly executed according to the Commandment.

The animals work all that year to rebuild the windmill. Napoleon is more distant and grandiose than ever, traveling around the farm escorted by the guard of dogs, keeping himself in lofty isolation from the others, and being addressed formally as "our Leader, Comrade Napoleon." The animals outdo each other in fulsome praise of Napoleon and his outstanding ability and wisdom in all areas. Minimus, the Poet, even composes a hymn praising Napoleon.

Napoleon engages in complicated negotiations with Frederick of Pinchfield and Pilkington of Foxwood. Finally, the windmill is repaired. Suddenly Napoleon veers toward Frederick and agrees to sell him some timber. But the money which Frederick pays for the lumber turns out to be counterfeit, and at the same moment as the animals find out this deception, Frederick attacks the Farm and blows up the new windmill. Frederick's invading forces are driven off at heavy cost, but the windmill is totally destroyed. This is a terrible disaster for Animal Farm, because it is the second time the windmill has been smashed. Napoleon converts the tragedy into a victory, which he and his associates celebrate by getting drunk and having a wild party in the farmhouse. Their carousing is barely concealed from the farm animals.

The Fifth Commandment had said: "No animal shall drink alcohol." But as Muriel points out when she reads it again, the wording is: "No animal shall drink alcohol to excess."

COMMENT

The changed wording of the Commandments is done secretly. Squealer is nearly caught changing the Commandments when he falls from a ladder in the middle of the night near the wall on which the Commandments are inscribed. The animals who rush to the place where Squealer is lying see a paint pot beside the broken ladder. However, the dogs immediately make a ring around Squealer and escort him back to the farmhouse. The onlookers cannot quite figure this out, so Squealer escapes discovery. This incident shows that truth is whatever the Party or the Leader say it is at the moment.

It also shows how propaganda subverts reality. Squealer is head of propaganda for Napoleon. He is the apologist, the one who explains the shifts in Napoleon's policies in such a way that the animals can accept them even if they cannot understand them. Notice that Orwell gives Squealer almost no personality, since he exists only to give voice to facts, figures, and the dictator's commands. This is also shown by the change in Snowball's honor in Battle of the Cowshed, when he had been awarded the medal of "Animal Hero, First Class." Gradually this had become the title "Animal Hero, Second Class." But even this is taken away from Snowball, and in this chapter Napoleon proclaims that Snowball had been a traitor from the very beginning.

Stalin's followers in other countries just prior to the German attack on Russia were hard put to justify the shifts in position of the Soviet Government in the period 1938–41, in which Stalin concluded a non-aggression pact with Hitler. The Nazi-Soviet pact shocked the friends and admirers of the Soviets perhaps more than any other single incident since the Russian Revolution. Orwell mirrors the Nazi-Soviet pact in the counterfeit bank notes that Frederick used to pay for the lumber.

There are certain details in the satire of Chapter Eight which bear additional comment. Napoleon has ordered the propaganda-carrying pigeons (the Comintern, or Stalinist agency for spreading revolution into other countries) to stay away from Foxwood, when Napoleon was negotiating with Pilkington of Foxwood for the sale of the lumber. But then Napoleon has a change of mind, and throws his attention to Frederick—just as Stalin had cultivated the English, then switched to Hitler, and then had loudly called for and received help from England.

The Battle of the Windmill, which destroys most of what the Farm has built up since the Revolution, corresponds to the Nazi attack on Russia. Just as the Germans alienated the Russians by brutal treatment, so Frederick of Pinchfield, by his destruction of the windmill, hits the animals hard. During the Second World War, Stalin held the the revolutionary aspect of Communism—the emphasis on world-revolution and the class-struggle—in abeyance. He did this to avoid alienating Britain and America, who were supplying him with vast quantities of war materials. Orwell represents this by the instructions Napoleon gives to the pigeons.

The drunken party at the end of this chapter represents the special privileges which the leaders of Animal Farm have assumed with no authority from the "comrades." So it is, implies Orwell, and so it will always be: once a revolution is made and leaders get into power, they will be corrupted.

CHAPTER NINE

Now the animals work furiously again, although the older Revolutionaries are somewhat worn down. Some are getting close to the retirement which had been established when Jones had been driven out. Of course, no animal had actually retired and received a pension, but there had been lean years where much work had to be done to consolidate the Animal Revolution.

Meanwhile, another hard winter comes, and even though Squealer is always ready to recite lists of production "victories," still the fact is that rations are once more reduced—except for the rations of the pigs, and their guards and auxiliaries, the dogs. The Farm does slightly better economically, however, though the food shortages remain. Spontaneous demonstrations are held and the animals are ordered to participate. There are processions and colored shirts. The sheep, Napoleon's greatest devotees, chant loudly. Animal Farm is proclaimed a Republic and a President is elected, but Napoleon is the only candidate and he is elected unanimously. Meanwhile, Moses gives out more information about the Sugarcandy Mountains. Napoleon and Squealer release more documents about Snowball's treasonable activities; the papers "prove" him to have been on the side of the humans from the very beginning of the Revolution. By now the animals, even those who knew Snowball well at the time of the Revolution, have only dim memories of him and believe what they are told.

Boxer has spent his strength in the service of the Farm. One of the mainstays of Napoleon's regime, the old horse suffers a complete physical breakdown. His lungs are weakening after the years of hard labor. He had been looking forward to retirement, but when he collapses, Squealer calls an "ambulance." In the middle of the day, when the other animals are at work, it comes. Benjamin, who can read, is terrified; this is the first time anyone can remember seeing him so disturbed.

He reads aloud to the other animals what is written on the side of the "ambulance": "Alfred Simmonds, Horse Slaughterer and Glue Boiler, Willingdon. Dealer in Hides and Bone-Meal."

Boxer is being taken to the knacker's to be made into glue and meal. Squealer tells the animals Boxer died in the hospital, his last words being "Napoleon is always right." Later that night, the pigs, having obtained money from some unexplained source, purchase a case of whiskey and engage in a drunken party capped by a tremendous brawl amongst them.

COMMENT

Here we see the indifference of all totalitarian regimes to those who serve them faithfully. Boxer had trusted Napoleon up to the last moment and yet was most brutally betrayed.

Squealer represents the totalitarian State-controlled press. Squealer uses euphemisms to achieve his aim. For example, "readjustment" is used in place of "reduction" to describe what has happened to the daily ration. "Ambulance" for "horse-slaughterer's van" is an especially grim jest. Squealer gives out limitless revisions of reality in the form of lists of goods and indexes showing that the animals have a much higher standard of living than they ever did under Jones. But no matter how encouraging the lists are, the animals, other than the pigs and dogs, are still short of food. One class of exploiters has simply been replaced by another. The ordinary inhabitants of the Farm, Orwell says, have seen little or no improvement in their lot.

Class-distinctions have become much more evident on the Farm, although in theory the Farm was a "classless society" as Marx had stated would be the case under Communism. Small distinctions are magnified: animals meeting one of the pigs on a narrow path are required to stand aside; the pigs are granted the privilege of wearing green ribbons on their tails on Sundays. The gestures of subservience to the pigs and especially to Comrade Napoleon and the green ribbons do not square with the final Commandment, as even the less intelligent animals perceive. Finally, the spontaneous demonstrations are a trapping of totalitarianism. These demonstrations are carefully organized and disciplined because a totalitarian leader cannot afford to have wild manifestations of popular support and hero-worship getting out of hand.

It is very strange to the animals that the pigs tolerate Moses's stories of the Sugarcandy Mountains awaiting them after death. The pigs even supply Moses with a ration of beer although he is not required to do physical work. Under totalitarian rule, religion was acceptable because it made people content with their lot in life. Therefore, Moses is simply another for keeping the citizenry quiet.

As the chapter ends, very few of the "old guard," the original revolutionaries, are left and the memories of those who remain are dimmed with time. Napoleon may thus feel safe in making his final move.

CHAPTER TEN

There are many new inhabitants of the Farm now, none of whom can remember the Revolution. The Farm is now run far more efficiently. The windmill has been rebuilt and is being used for milling corn rather than its original purpose, providing electricity to make life easier for the animals. A second windmill is to be built, accelerating the industrialization of the Farm. Ordinary animals work just as hard as ever, as Napoleon believes that vacations and heated and lighted stalls were "contrary to the spirit of Animalism." While the Farm seems richer, the ordinary animals are no richer—the surplus wealth seems to go to the hands of the pigs and dogs, just as in the old days it went to Mr. Jones. But the greatest shock is to come.

One day the animals see a terrifying sight: Squealer walking on his hind legs. Soon all of the pigs appear from the farmhouse, walking like humans. And then Napoleon appears on two legs and carrying a whip. The sheep begin bleating: "Four legs good, two legs better!" No other animal dares to say anything. As this seems such a radical departure from Animalism, Clover asks Benjamin to take her to the wall the Commandments are written. But instead of the Seven Commandments, all that Benjamin sees written on the wall is this:

ALL ANIMALS ARE EQUAL
BUT SOME ANIMALS ARE MORE EQUAL THAN OTHERS.

Shortly thereafter, the neighboring farmers come at Napoleon's invitation to a banquet to see the Farm for themselves. Peering in at the festivities, the ordinary animals see Napoleon, Mr. Pilkington, and other assorted pigs and humans quarreling violently. But it is impossible for the onlookers to say which of those who are quarreling are men and which are pigs.

COMMENT

In this last chapter, Orwell shows us that the wheel has come full circle—the regime which has been set up by the pigs in the name of the Animal Revolution is at least as bad, if not worse, as the regime under Jones. It is more efficient, it is true, because Jones was so undisciplined and pleasure-loving that he could not run the Farm well. And technology had advanced in the meantime, but it is hard to establish whether the pigs could really take much credit for this.

All of the Commandments had been rewritten, until finally they are compressed into one: the most famous line in Animal Farm and a perfect summation of Orwell's satiric theme and purpose: All Animals Are Equal But Some Animals Are More Equal Than Others. What began as heaven on earth, the promise of a new life, has ended in despair and heartache. The alteration of the final and most important commandment suggests that there is something in human nature that will prevent people from ever achieving utopia. Ideals, hard work, and good intentions are not sufficient. The strong will triumph over the weak and utopia remains but a dream.

The banquet signifies England's cooperation with Stalin during the Second World War. But at the banquet, it could already be discerned that there was likely to be a conflict of interest between Russia and the Western Allies. Russia had been idealized by many outsiders during the War because of the tremendous battle it had made against Hitler.

As the animals creep away from eavesdropping on the banquet, they hear a quarrel and harsh words. Napoleon and Pilkington have been playing at cards, which symbolizes the cooperation of Russia and the West during the Second World War. But now each side accuses the other of playing the ace of spades simultaneously, and as there is only one such card they cannot both have it. The book ends with the humans and the animal quarreling over what both desire but neither should have—ace of spades (world domination).

CHARACTER ANALYSES

FARMER JONES

Farmer Jones represents the last Russian Tsar, Nicholas II, and the Tsarist system which had broken down in Russia. At the most fundamental level Jones symbolizes the breakdown of the old European monarchist order in most countries —"the decay of ability in the ruling class"—as Orwell had stated in another essay.

Jones is incompetent and selfish; he often becomes so drunk that he forgets about the animals. Jones is driven off the Farm by the hungry animals' spontaneous revolt.

NAPOLEON

Napoleon is the novel's central character. It is probable that Orwell chose the pig's name because the historical Napoleon, Emperor of the French, became supreme ruler only a few years after the hopes for Liberty, Equality, Fraternity, and the Rights of Man had been embodied in the French Revolution. Yet Napoleon became as autocratic as the former King of France within a very short time. Power corrupts, and the pig-Napoleon who figures so prominently in *Animal Farm* is just repeating a pattern. Such was the fate of all Revolutions, Orwell suggests.

Napoleon of *Animal Farm,* like Stalin, is presented as intellectually less nimble than his arch-rival Snowball (Trotsky). He is not particularly creative, but he does know when to take over an idea from someone else. This is shown when he takes Snowball's plan for the windmill and makes it his own. He also knows how to build an apparatus for controlling others, as did Stalin. He uses assistants, such as Squealer, who may be more clever than he is—but he knows their limitations and how to keep them in line. Napoleon is characterized by great force of will and personality and total lack of scruples (as witness his shameful treatment of the faithful

Boxer). He also has some uncontrolled personal habits which he is careful to keep out of sight of the masses, though his trusted followers who are dependent on his good will know about them.

SNOWBALL

Snowball is Napoleon's rival, and he is much more creative, clever, and inventive. However, he lacks the kind of ability for intrigue which would have enabled him to build a powerful political machine to dominate the Farm. He represents Trotsky in terms of Orwell's satire on Russian history. But Snowball also represents the scapegoat, needed by every dictator. A dictator claims to be omnipotent and all-powerful. If this is so, how then can he have failures, such as the terrible fiasco of windmill's destruction and the payment for the timber in counterfeit notes? To admit that this was the Leader's fault would be to weaken his position. Therefore, Napoleon blames everything on Snowball, the scapegoat. The credulous animals believe him. Those who do not find it prudent to keep their opinions to themselves. Everything that goes wrong on the Farm is blamed on Snowball. Napoleon thus succeeds in creating a "devil," an adversary to satisfy the psychological need of his subjects to have an object on whom they may project their frustration at various failure.

OLD MAJOR

Old Major is the prophet of the Animal Revolution, who dies before the Revolution actually takes place. An idealist, a law-giver, and a spellbinding orator, he puts the idea of rebellion into the heads of the animals with a clever appeal backed by probable sincerity. A majestic-looking twelve-year-old pig, old Major has a wise and benevolent appearance, though his tushes have never been cut and look quite formidable and dangerous—as are his ideas. His is the dream of the Revolution, and he seems to represent Karl Marx, the most important historical theoretician of Marxism and Communism. Old Major is a sincere dreamer who leaves to others the task of carrying out the Revolution. These others corrupt old Major's ideas in a shift of power. Orwell implies that this is always the case.

Old Major can be seen to represent Lenin as well as Marx, as his successors are Napoleon and Snowball, who fight over the succession to power with the result that Snowball loses and is exiled. But Stalin and Trotsky were successors not to Marx directly, but to Lenin; and therefore old Major, in the historical satire, has the dual meaning. Old Major also represents all great thinkers who have changed the conditions of life with their ideas, even as their ideas were taken over by followers who perverted these ideas to their own advantage. Old Major, then, though he appears only briefly in the first chapter of *Animal Farm,* is a very important character.

SQUEALER

Squealer is Napoleon's "mouthpiece," corresponding to a totalitarian minister of propaganda such as Dr. Goebbels under Hitler. He makes bad look good, and is always ready with lists of figures showing that the animals were constantly becoming better off than they had been the year before.

Squealer does much of Napoleon's dirty work, and it is clear that he exercises "reality control" over the other animals. Squealer was once nearly caught in the act. One night after a drunken carouse in the farmhouse, Squealer was found insensible under the place where the Commandments were painted, a broken ladder and a paint pot nearby. But the dogs surrounded him and led him off, so the animals did not suspect the truth. If they did, they kept quiet about it. Squealer conceals the truth from the animals. In doing so he perverts language, using euphemisms instead of clear terms to make that which is brutal or treacherous palatable. Squealer ultimately becomes so fat that he has difficulty seeing.

THE DOGS

The dogs are a group of fierce hounds which Napoleon had trained himself as his own guards, taking them under his protection at an early age. They corresponded to the Secret Police and to the other apparatus of terrorism and repression in a totalitarian state.

MR. PILKINGTON OF FOXWOOD

Mr. Pilkington of Foxwood is one of the two closest neighbors to Animal Farm. Foxwood is a large but rather neglected farm, rather overgrown by woodland. Mr. Pilkington is an easygoing gentleman who does not have quite the vices of Jones but who spends much time hunting and fishing. Pilkington represents England and the British Government. At the end of the book Pilkington cooperates with Napoleon. Then they have a severe quarrel, corresponding to the widening split between Stalin and the Western Allies.

MR. FREDERICK OF PINCHFIELD

Mr. Frederick of Pinchfield corresponds to the German nation. Frederick is tough and shrewd and quarrelsome: he is always involved in lawsuits (wars) and drives hand bargains. Pinchfield is a smaller but better-kept and more efficiently run farm than is Foxwood. Frederick makes an agreement to buy some timber from Napoleon, which corresponds to the Russo-German nonaggression pact before the Second World War. Then he double-crosses Napoleon by paying for the timber in counterfeit notes. At the same time he attacks Animal Farm and dynamites the windmill on which the animals had lavished such effort. But the ordinary citizens of the Farm, inspired by Boxer's strength, rally and drive Frederick off the farm.

MR. WHYMPER

Mr. Whymper is an attorney Napoleon hired as intermediary between the Farm and the humans. He represents the middleman, the necessary business relationships which must take place even between states which are hostile to one another. In the process he slyly enriches himself. The animals do not trust him, but their egos are fed by seeing a human, one of their former masters, serving them.

MOSES

Moses is a raven who does not work as the other animals do on the Farm. Originally Mr. Jones's special pet, he is a spy and talebearer. He tries to make the animals resigned to their lot by telling them of a mysterious country called Sugarcandy Mountain where all animals go when they die. Some of the animals believed these stories. When Jones is forced to flee, Moses follows him, but soon reappears on the Farm. The pigs accept him and give him a ration to support him even though he still does no work. The pigs find him a useful ally, because the story of the Sugarcandy Mountains keeps the animals quiet. He symbolizes the Orthodox Church and organized religion.

BENJAMIN

Benjamin is the donkey, a cynic who does not believe that anything will be different once the Revolution has come. He is the oldest animal on the farm, and has the worst temper. However, he works hard although he is a "loner." Further, he is devoted to Boxer, whose strength and dedication he respects. He tries to save Boxer near the end, when Boxer is hauled off to the knacker, but he is unsuccessful. His pessimistic view about the outcome of the Revolution corresponds in some particulars to Orwell's own view of the failure of Marxism and Communism.

BOXER

Boxer is an enormously strong horse who performs prodigies of physical strength. He is not very bright, and is ultimately tricked to his death by Napoleon once his strength has given out in the service of Animal Farm. He believes in the Revolution, and coins two personal slogans; "I will work harder," and "Comrade Napoleon is always right." He fights bravely during the Battle of the Cowshed, and Napoleon's treatment of him is the worst betrayal. He represents the unthinking masses; he is really loyal more to the Farm than to Napoleon, but he is not clever enough to protect himself against Napoleon.

CLOVER

Clover is a mare, also a hard worker and not very bright. Like Boxer, she allows herself to be tricked again and again by the pigs. She knows dimly that things have not worked out quite in the way that the Revolution had promised, but she cannot perceive why. Clover is Boxer's friend and tries to save him from his fate.

MURIEL

Muriel is a white goat. She is able to read somewhat better than most of the animals. As a result, she reads the Commandments for them.

MOLLIE

Mollie is a pleasure-loving white mare who draws Mr. Jones's trap. She succumbs to the attractions of "bourgeois society" and would probably be called a "reactionary."

THE CAT

The cat is concerned for his own survival and personal gain. This is shown when he votes on both sides of the question raised at the meeting with old Major.

THE SHEEP

The sheep are the mindless masses, who can only bleat slogans in support of Comrade Napoleon.

BLUEBELL AND JESSIE

Bluebell and Jessie are two dogs, whose puppies are taken by Napoleon at an early age and "conditioned" so that he may make them his guards and Secret Police.

CRITICAL COMMENTARY

In 1947, George Orwell said that *Animal Farm* was "the first book in which I tried, with full consciousness of what I was doing, to fuse political and artistic purpose into one whole" (*Dictionary of Literary Biography* 15, p. 419). Critics are in virtual agreement that Orwell's "fairy tale" is a remarkable effective integration of a political message within a unified fictional narrative. As one critic remarked, "The use of the fable, the simplicity of style, and the notable absence of a narrative or authorial voice provide *Animal Farm* with the potential for a mythic quality that engages a deeper level of consciousness than either realistic fiction or the essay." The novel is also regarded as a masterpiece of English prose. Orwell's ability to perceive the social effects of political theories inspired social critic and writer Irving Howe to call him "the greatest moral force in English letters during the past several decades."

The search for a publisher for *Animal Farm* took over a year and a half; the novel was rejected by many publishing companies on the grounds that it was too harsh a criticism of the Soviet Union, then an ally of the British government. One British publisher said that the novel was too grim in its outlook. An American publisher turned it down because animal stories were not popular in the United States. Once the novel was finally published, however, it was an immediate success, earning enthusiastic reviews and selling out its first edition in only a few months. Since its initial publication, *Animal Farm* has sold more than nine million copies and has been translated into dozens of languages.

Further, Orwell's prose has become a model for students of writing because of its precision, clarity, and vividness. Many critics contend that in *Animal Farm* Orwell achieved his ideal of prose like "a window pane" through which the reader can examine a topic without encountering an obtrusive authorial presence. The animal fable eliminated the need for Orwell to intrude with his own comments, because any moral is implicit in the fable and stands on its own.

Many ideas from Orwell's fiction have become part of the modern imagination. This is especially true of *Animal Farm.* Critic Richard I. Smyer has said that "Orwell belongs to a small group of twentieth-century writers whose fictional works have influenced the thinking of readers who are only slightly interested in imaginative literature. The seventh commandment of Animalism, with its final perversion—"All animals are equal, but some animals are more equal than others"—is perhaps as widely familair as the catchphrases from *1984* that have become part of the mass consciousness of the late twentieth century.

A SELECTION OF VIEWS ON ANIMAL FARM

LIONEL TRILLING

In "George Orwell and the Politics of Truth," critic Lionel Trilling said that Orwel was an honest and honorable man as well as an honest man of letters. For Professor Trilling, Orwell was a committed man, in the sense that he lived his vision, as have Thoreau, Mark Twain, Walt Whitman, among major American writers of the past century. Orwell, in fact, was more modern than these; he was "engaged" in the sense that some of the Existentialists have been engaged and committed to political thought and action for the betterment of human life, whether or not they believed at the time that betterment was possible. Professor Trilling claims that Orwell's writing was directly related to the promotion of human decency.

JOHN ATKINS

In *George Orwell,* Atkins accepts the interpretation of the satire of *Animal Farm* as existing on a number of levels, including the history of Stalinist Russia. According to Atkins, *Animal Farm* contains most of Orwell's major ideas about politics. Atkins follows the main line of interpretation of *Animal Farm* concerning levels of satire, from the childhood fable to the serious, even profound, political commentary to commentary on human nature and the fate of revolutions.

SIR RICHARD REES

In *George Orwell: Fugitive from the Camp of Victory*, Rees explains that Orwell's view of the common man had undoubtedly become darker after the early 1940s, in part due to his deepening pessimism on the basis of his own experience. Orwell had made reference to his experience in Spain, in which the POUM perished because they came into conflict with Stalinism. All they wanted was to get on with the fight against the common enemy of the Spanish Republic. In *Animal Farm* the ordinary residents of the Farm, once they have overthrown Jones, allow themselves to be hoodwinked and then enslaved by a gang of pigs. And Rees attributes this pessimistic conclusion to Orwell's own experiences, primarily in Spain, and to his reading of history in the light of such experience.

CHRISTOPHER HOLLIS

Hollis considers *Animal Farm* to be a great work of art rather than simply an ephemeral political tract. Orwell had said that *Animal Farm* had been a conscious fusion of political purpose and artistic purpose. Mr. Hollis shares the view held by others that in *Animal Farm* Orwell attained such perfection of technique within the limits of his political purpose that the book deserves to be called a classic, and will probably endure as such.

Further, Hollis believes *Animal Farm* to be a satire on all totalitarianism, and not simply communism.

RICHARD J. VOORHEES

In *The Paradox of George Orwell*, Professor Voorhees claims because Orwell made *Animal Farm* sound too convincing on the concrete level that it has largely been relegated to the status of a children's work. Further, he thought Arthur Koestler's *Darkness at Noon* to be a more convincing critique of totalitarianism than *Animal Farm*. But he gives little evidence to support his contention.

ESSAY QUESTIONS AND ANSWERS

QUESTION

What do the animals think of Boxer?

ANSWER

Boxer is the farm's hard-working and fiercely strong draft horse. He is an enormous beast, nearly eighteen hands high, and as strong as any two horses put together. A white stripe down his nose gives him a somewhat stupid look, and in fact he is not a very intelligent creature. Nonetheless, he is universally respected on the farm for his steadiness of character and tremendous powers of work. Everyone admires Boxer, and their admiration only increases after the Revolution.

He had worked hard when Jones owned the farm, but now he seems like three horses in one. There are days when all the work on the farm seemed to rest on his broad shoulders. From morning until night he was pushing and pulling. He could always be found at the spot where the work was the most difficult. He even made arrangements with one of the cockerels to call him in the morning half an hour earlier than anyone else so he could put in some volunteer labor at whatever seemed to be most needed. His answer to every setback, every problem, was the same: "I will work harder." This became his personal motto.

QUESTION

What is the "Battle of the Cowshed"?

ANSWER

The Battle of the Cowshed (Chapter Four) starts when Jones and all his men, supported with half a dozen other men from Foxwood and Pinchfield, attempt to recapture Animal Farm. Jones's assault was not a surprise to the animals; they had long anticipated such an invasion. Snowball had studied an old book on campaign strategy to prepare for the assault and was in charge of the defense. As a result of Snowball's careful preparations and outstanding leadership, the animals perform like a disciplined army. They set aside any concern for personal safety. Snowball in particular performs with great bravery, dashing straight for Jones. The farmer sees the pig heading toward him and fires. Snowball is grazed by Jones's bullets but he does not stop for a minute. He flings his entire weight against Jones's legs and the farmer is hurled into a pile of dung. The animals successfully repulse the attack and Snowball is given the military decoration "Animal Hero, First Class" for his exemplary leadership and bravery. Later in the novel, when Snowball has been driven from the farm by Napoleon, the latter will twist the events of the Battle of the Cowshed to accuse Snowball of cowardice and deception.

QUESTION

What causes the windmill to collapse at the end of Chapter Six? How does Napoleon explain the collapse of the windmill?

ANSWER

After years of brutal toil, the windmill is finally finished. But the winter proves the hardest yet. Raging winds and violent gales rock the farm. The storms are so strong that they destroy the windmill, smashing it to the ground. In Chapter Seven, the humans on neighboring farms state that the walls of the windmill were not as thick as they should have been, making it inevitable that it would be destroyed in a storm.

Using the destruction of the windmill to serve his own ends, Napoleon claims that Snowball crept back to the farm under cover of night and smashed the windmill. Napoleon levies a death sentence on Snowball and pledges a full bushel of apples to any animal who can bring Snowball to Animal Farm to stand trial and be executed.

QUESTION

What happens to Boxer at the end of the novel?

ANSWER

Late one evening in the summer, a sudden rumor flies around the farm that something has happened to Boxer. He had gone out by himself to drag a load of stone to the windmill. When some of the animals go to the windmill to investigate, they discover that Boxer has collapsed. He is lying on his side and he cannot get up. About half the animals on the farm rush to Boxer's side. The huge horse is bleeding from the mouth; his strength is gone. Some of the other animals summon Squealer to help. Squealer offers Comrade Napoleon's support and says that arrangements have been made to take Boxer to the hospital at Willingdon. The animals are uneasy at this, for almost none of them had ever left the farm. They do not like to think that their sick friend will be treated by humans, but Squealer allays their fears. For two days, Boxer stays in his stall. Clover gives him some of the pink medicine the pigs had found in the medicine chest. Benjamin keeps the flies away.

However, Clover and Benjamin can only be with Boxer after working hours. In the middle of the day, a van comes to take Boxer away. On the side of the van is written: "Alfred Simmonds, Horse Slaughterer and Glue Boiler, Willingdon. Dealer in Hides and Bone-Meal. Kennels Supplied." Only Benjamin realizes what this means: Boxer is being taken to the knacker's. The farm's hardest worker and most devoted follower is being made into glue and dog food.

QUESTION

How has the farm changed by the end of the novel?

ANSWER

The farm has now become a place of terror and slaughter. Animals are killing other animals as Napoleon orders executions to purge the farm of malcontents and solidify his power.

While Jones had regularly killed animals for meat, under human rule no animal had ever killed another animal. Further, none of the animals dares to speak its mind; fierce dogs roam everywhere. The animals watch their friends and family being torn to pieces after confessing to shocking crimes.

QUESTION

How is *Animal Farm* a satire of the Communist revolution in Russia?

ANSWER

Animal Farm is a satire, using the device of the animal fable. As such, each of the animals is used to represent a particular aspect of Communism in the former Soviet Union.

Old Major represents Karl Marx; old Major's ideas on the oppression of animals by human beings is Marxist doctrine. The men stand for Marx's capitalists, while the animals are the working men and women. Major can also be seen as Lenin, before the Revolution. Mr. Jones is Czar Nicholas II, overthrown by the Communists. The animals' actual revolution is the Russian Revolution of 1917. Napoleon is Stalin, and Snowball is Trotsky. Squealer is Stalin's propaganda agent. His function is to distort reality and to rewrite history in such a way that written documents (e.g. the Seven Commandments of Animalism) are constantly changed in order to bring them into conformity with Party policy retroactively.

Pilkington and Foxwood Farm stand for Great Britain, while Frederick and Pinchfield Farm stand for Germany. Orwell parallels Russia's relationship to these countries in Napoleon's dealings with them. The Battle of the Cowshed, the first invasion of Animal Farm, is the anti-revolutionary invasion of the new Soviet Russia by the West; the Battle of the Windmill, the second invasion, represents the German invasion of Russia during World War II.

The repeated attempts to build the windmill refer to Stalin's Five-Year Plans. The horrifying repression of Stalin's rule is shown in the gradual enslavement of the animals, his purges, trials, and phony confessions. Finally, the Teheran Conference is alluded to in the novel's last scene. Napoleon sitting down with the men at the drunken party parallels Stalin's meeting with representatives from the West.

QUESTION

Since Napoleon and the other pigs declare that Moses's stories about Sugarcandy Mountain are all lies, why do they let the raven stay on the farm, not make him work, and give him an allowance of a gill of beer a day?

ANSWER

Moses, the raven, symbolizes organized religion. Napoleon and the pigs let Moses stay because they think that religion will dull the other animals to their pain. This is Karl Marx's argument that religion is the "opiate of the masses." Moses is helpful to the pigs as long as he does not get in the way of Napoleon's plans for the animals.

QUESTION

Why does Napoleon return the farm to its original name, Manor Farm?

ANSWER

By the end of the novel, the pigs look and act like human beings. They even carry whips, the dreaded symbol of human oppression. In short, the pigs have put on all the physical and social characteristics of humans. It is therefore fitting that "Animal Farm" revert to its original name "Manor Farm," because everything is just the same as it always was, except for one thing: the animals have experienced freedom but have had it snatched away.

QUESTION

What is the novel's theme or main idea?

ANSWER

On one level, Orwell was specifically satirizing the failure of Communism in Russia. But on a large plane, Orwell's theme is revolution betrayed. The novel explores the ways in which our best intentions cannot succeed against selfishness, hypocrisy, and lust for power. Orwell suggests that humanity can never achieve paradise because of our nature. He traces how the ordinary person often unwittingly supports his own undoing.

QUESTION

How are the animals symbols or types rather than three-dimensional characters?

ANSWER

In an animal fable, each character must function both as an animal and as the representation of a human trait. Boxer, for example, is literally a tremendously strong and kind horse. He also represents the patient, plodding masses, the ordinary people who work faithfully to the limits of their strength and then die without complaint. Clover is a mare who represents motherly concern. Benjamin is a donkey; he symbolizes the skeptic who believes that human nature will never change. Mollie is a pretty young mare; she stands for personal vanity and frivolity.

QUESTION

What is the relationship between *Animal Farm* and *1984*?

ANSWER

The two books are both Orwell's masterpieces, although he is probably better known for the latter. Both deal with "the central question: how to prevent power from being abused," to quote Orwell. Each of the books employs a different satiric method in pursuit of this end; *Animal Farm* is a beast-fable while *1984* is anti-Utopia.

There are many similarities between the two works. In both, there is an originally idealistic Revolution which has become corrupt and an all-powerful Leader who has seized and maintained power by force, guile, and terrorism. In both cases, the general population is oppressed and terrorized so that any expressions of independent opinion may have the most dire consequences. Finally, in both Orwell shows the perversion of human equality and fraternity into a sinister myth bearing no relation to truth.

Animal Farm, unlike *1984*, may be read for entertainment; it would be possible for children to read *Animal Farm* without any awareness of the political satire, just as *Gulliver's Travels* is often read on this level.

QUESTION

What is the function of the four human characters who have "speaking parts" in *Animal Farm*?

ANSWER

These are Farmer Jones, Lawyer Whymper, Pilkington of Foxwood, and Frederick of Pinchfield. Orwell used all four as foils to contrast the animal characters. The humans and the animals are presented as being motivated by the same unworthy drives and wishes. Orwell implies that one may expect humans to live according to reason and morality more than animals. But at least in the field of political affairs and especially of international relations, the law of the jungle prevails. Men are no better than animals in this respect, yet they should be better if the long history of human civilization means anything.

QUESTION

Relate Lord Acton's statement "Power corrupts, and absolute power corrupts absolutely" to *Animal Farm*.

ANSWER

In *Animal Farm*, as in pre-1917 Russia, there is a power-vacuum, because Farmer Jones is unwilling or unable to exercise his power. The animals seize power out of idealistic motives. But immediately the jockeying for power and position begins. Along the way, Snowball is forced out and Napoleon becomes supreme. Instead of exercising power fairly, Napoleon uses his position to obtain more and more special privileges for his "class" and himself, using the agency of Squealer to justify this seizure. Orwell implies that all revolutions become corrupt.

SELECTED BIBLIOGRAPHY

WORKS BY GEORGE ORWELL

Orwell, George. *Animal Farm*. New York: Harcourt, Brace & World, Inc. 1946. Reprinted in Signet Edition, New American Library, N.Y. 1956.

______. *Burmese Days*. New York: Harcourt, Brace & World, Inc. 1934; reprinted in Popular Library, New York, 1958.

______. *A Clergyman's Daughter*. American Edition: New York: Harcourt, Brace and Co., Inc. 1935.

______. *A Collection of Essays*. Garden City, N.Y.: Doubleday and Co., Doubleday Anchor Books, 1954.

______. *Coming Up for Air*. New York: Harcourt, Brace & World, Inc., 1939. Reprinted 1950: Avon Publishing Co., Inc., New York.

______. *Critical Essays*. London: Secker and Warburg, 1946.

______. *Down and Out in Paris and London*. Harcourt, Brace & World, Inc., 1933. Reprinted by Avon Publications, New York, N.Y.

______. *England, Your England and Other Essays*. London: Secker and Warburg, 1953.

______. *Homage to Catalonia*. Boston: Harcourt, Brace & World, Inc. Reprinted by Beacon Press, 1952. Intro. by Lionel Trilling.

______. *Keep the Aspidistra Flying*. New York: Harcourt, Brace & World, Inc. 1956; reprinted in Popular Library, New York, 1957.

_______. *1984.* New York: Harcourt, Brace & World, Inc., 1949. Reprinted by Signet Books: The New American Library of World Literature, Inc., New York, N.Y., 1950.

_______. *The Orwell Reader: Fiction, Essays, and Reportage.* Ed. by Richard H. Rovere. New York: Harcourt, Brace & World, Inc., Harvest Books, 1956.

_______. *The Road to Wigan Pier.* New York, N.Y.: Harcourt, Brace and Co., 1958. (First Published in England, 1937; see the Introduction by Victor Gollancz also printed in the 1958 American edition.)

_______. *Second Thoughts on James Burnham.* (Magazine article in *Polemic,* Vol. III; printed separately by Socialist Book Center, 158 Strand, London, July, 1946. A very important pamphlet for the study of the relation between Burnham's ideas and the satire of both *1984* and *Animal Farm.*)

BIOGRAPHICAL AND CRITICAL WORKS

Alldritt, Keith. *The Making of George Orwell: A Literary History*. New York: St. Martin's Press, 1969.

Atkins, John. *George Orwell: A Literary and Biographical Study*. New York: Frederick Ungar Publishing Co., 1954.

Beadle, Gordon. "George Orwell and the Spanish Civil War," *Duquesne Review*, 16 (Spring 1971), pp. 3–16.

Brander, Laurence. *George Orwell*. London: Longmans, Green, 1954.

Calder, Jenni. *Chronicles of Conscience: A Study of George Orwell and Arthur Koestler*. London: Secker & Warburg, 1968.

Connolly, Cyril. *Enemies of Promise*. New York: Macmillan, 1948.

Crick, Bernack. *George Orwell: A Life*. Boston: Little, Brown, 1980.

Fyvel, T.R. "George Orwell and Eric Blair: Glimpses of a Dual Life." *Encounter*, 13, July 1959, pp. 60–65.

Gross, Miriam. ed. *The World of George Orwell*. New York: Simon and Schuster, 1971.

Highet, Gilbert. *A Clerk of Oxenford*. New York: Oxford Univ. Press, 1954.

Hollis, Christopher. *A Study of George Orwell: The Man and His Works*. London: Hollis & Carter, 1956.

Hopkinson, Henry Thomas. *George Orwell*. Published for the British Council and the National Book League by Longmans, Green and Co. No. 39 in the series, *Writers and Their Works*, London, 1961.

Howe, Irving. "Orwell: History as Nightmare," in *Politics and the Novel*. New York: Horizon, 1956, pp. 235–251.

Kubal, David L. *Outside the Whale: George Orwell's Art and Politics*. Notre Dame: University of Notre Dame Press, 1972.

Lee. Robert A. *Orwell's Fiction*. Notre Dame: University of Notre Dame Press, 1969.

Meyers, Jeffrey, ed. *George Orwell: The Critical Heritage*. London: Routledge & Kegan Paul, 1975.

Rahv, Philip. "The Unfuture of Utopia," *Partisan Review*, 16, July 1949, pp. 743–749.

Rees, Sir Richard. *George Orwell: Fugitive from the Camp of Victory*. Carbondale, Illinois: Southern Illinois University Press, 1961.

Stansky, Peter and William Abrahams. *The Unknown Orwell*. New York: Knopf, 1972.

Trilling, Lionel. "George Orwell and the Politics of Truth." *Commentary*, March, 1952; reprinted in *The Opposing Self*, New York: Viking Press, Compass Books, 1955.

Voorhees, Richard J. *The Paradox of George Orwell*. West Lafayette, Indiana: Purdue University Studies, Humanistic Series, 1961.

SUGGESTED INTRODUCTORY WORKS CONCERNING RUSSIAN HISTORY

Dallin, David J. *The Changing World of Soviet Russia.* New Haven: Yale University Press, 1956.

Dallin, David J. *From Purge to Coexistence.* Chicago: Henry Regnery Co., 1964.

Fainsod, Merle. *How Russia is Ruled.* Revised Edition: Cambridge, Mass., Harvard University Press, 1963.

Fischer, Louis. *The Life and Death of Stalin.* 1st ed. New York: Harper and Co., 1953.

Fischer, Louis. *The Life of Lenin.* New York and London: Harper and Row, 1964.

Mendel, Arthur P. *Essential Works of Marxism.* New York: Bantam Books (SC 125), 1961.

Stalin, Josef V. *Foundation of Leninism.* New York: International Publishers, 1932.

Trotsky, Leon. *Stalin: An Appraisal of the Man and His Influence.* Translated and edited by C. Malamuth. New York: Grosset and Dunlap, The Universal Library, 1941.

Wilson, Edmund. *To the Finland Station: A Study in the Writing and Acting of History.* New York, 1940; reprinted 1953 by Doubleday Anchor Books.

Wolfe, Bertram D. *Three Who Made a Revolution: A Biographical History.* New York: The Dial Press, 1948.

WORKS OF SPECIAL INTEREST IN
THE CRITICISM OF ORWELL'S POLITICAL THEORY

Burnham, James. *The Managerial Revolution.* New York: John Day and Co., 1941. (A work of great influence on Orwell's preoccupation with totalitarian forms of government and the way in which ruling hierarchies seize and maintain power. See also Orwell's own review of this book.)

Burnham, James. *The Machiavellians.* 1943. Reprinted 1963: Chicago: Gateway Editions, Henry Regnery Co. (A series of essays by Burnham developing some of his ideas about power, as illustrated in such political and social theorists as Dante, Machiavelli, Mosca, Sorel, and Pareto.)

Koestler. Arthur, *Darkness at Noon.* Reprinted 1958: New York, N.Y.: Signet Books, The New American Library. (An account of the Moscow Purge Trials of the 1930s in fictionalized form, of special interest for comparison with brainwashing and "reality control" in *Animal Farm.*)

SUGGESTED TOPICS
FOR FURTHER RESEARCH

1. Orwell's critique of Communism in *Animal Farm*.

2. Orwell's use of the beast-fable as a satiric instrument in *Animal Farm*.

3. Orwell's use of psychology in *Animal Farm*.

4. *Animal Farm, 1984*, and Orwell's presentation of brainwashing and thought control.

5. The relationship of *Animal Farm* to *1984*.
a. "Politics and the English Language" and *Animal Farm*.
b. *The Road to Wigan Pier* and *Animal Farm*.
c. *Coming Up for Air*.
d. *Homage to Catalonia*.
e. *Down and Out in Paris and London*.

6. Satirical techniques in *Animal Farm*.

7. The relation of Orwell's life to his writing.

8. Will *Animal Farm* endure as a classic, or is it too topical and local?

9. Snowball and Napoleon as satiric characters.

10. *Animal Farm* and the history of the Russian Revolution.

11. What are the political theses which Orwell expressed in *Animal Farm*?

12. Construct, from a reading of *Animal Farm* and other works of Orwell, a statement of his own political and social philosophy.

13. Which is the greater masterpiece: *1984* or *Animal Farm*?

14. The essential Marxist theses and their evident refutation in *Animal Farm*.

NOTES

NOTES

NOTES

NOTES

NOTES

NOTES

NOTES

NOTES

NOTES

NOTES

NOTES

NOTES

NOTES